Two Short Plays

By

Mary Louise Coulouris

And

Duncan Wallace

To all those who wished us well on the island of Hydra, Greece.

e: duncanwallace2000@yahoo.co.uk

Profile on LinkedIn

ISBN 978-1-4710-3317-9

<u>**Book-Face**</u>

A Tragi-Comedy in Two Parts

Cast

James: A hen-pecked husband.

Jean: His adventurous wife

Marvin: Son

Melinda: Their daughter

Dave: Computer repair man

Stephen: Paramedic

Annabel: Jean's friend

Stage Set

'Book-Face' is positioned in the wings and consists of two loudspeakers or two people using loudhailers on either side of the stage. The audience hears 'Yes' booming out in a loud voice from one side of the stage, then an interval, then 'No' at equal volume. This pattern is repeated at varying interval until the power and force of the statement cannot help but be absorbed by the audience. They are hypnotised by it and are on the verge of irritation.
The action begins. While the 'Yes;' and 'No' voices of Book-face have been sounding, some members of the cast or stage crew have moved the set (elevated window frame and chair) into position. The scene is a front room of an elegant late Georgian terrace on two floors with a tall wooden window frame and plain curtains in the background and a slightly fancy but functional armchair in the foreground facing towards the audience.

Act 1

Scene 1

Husband and wife.

The two children (Marvin and Matilda) are absent.

Jean, is deciding a number of things including what to wear at a parents evening they are both going to. Her husband, James, sits slumped in the armchair reading, nodding and shaking his head on and off and looking down. He is wearing a tired looking baggy and uninspiring lounge suit he has left on from work. Jean busies herself looking around the room and making the occasional dusting movement before beginning to ask questions of her husband. This scene is not unusual one for her and the way she looks for answers to her formidable list of queries is on the aggressive side. This is not atypical.

Jean It was unusual what happened to the Thomas's last week, don't you think? I mean asking for early retirement when he had such a nice job teaching and he seemed so happy though he was quiet in the classroom apparently and some of the kids took advantage of it, I think.

Well, that and his age, I suppose, I never could quite see why he looked so old when he was so much less, actually. Still, he's decided to stop, which is the main thing and probably wrong no doubt. I mean, who do they think they are?

Personally, he looks a bit old but he's well within retirement limits. They should promote him if anything, not encourage him to retire early. Whatever will the family do now? Then again, he may have decided to give up in his own best interests. It's whatever suits you these days, isn't it? What do you think James?

James Quite.....Yes.

Jean I mean, he never says much, it's always Tricia who does the talking and she seemed a little upset by it all. You could see it in her face although I'm never quite sure what it is that makes that lady go all out of sorts. It's a whole number of things I think and the light in that house of theirs isn't so good, not like our own house.

Not like our house is it James?

James Whose house?

Jean Our house. It's nothing like theirs. You work in the same profession and Tricia and I are very similar so you would think our two houses would contain the same ambience so to speak but they don't. Theirs is all dark and dingy like a cave isn't it?

James Whose house?

Jean Can you remember the last time we were there and Tricia put on some special things for dinner and we sat round and laughed about a few points of interest but we never laughed too strongly, did we? And there was all that stuff she had cleared away to the room where we left our coats. Left it out, she had, right there on the bed and all around the room. All higgeldy pickeldy, ornaments crammed onto the mantelpiece and odd bits of furniture cluttering the floor not to mention the bits and pieces strewn all over.

It was quite a revelation. A revelation to me by any measure, goodness only knows what you thought James, James?

James Yes dear. Quite...Quite a revelation I mean.

Jean It was always Tricia who did the talking, took all the decisions. Maybe she told him to take early retirement as well so she wouldn't have to walk the dog or something.

Well, I suppose he can do it more often now he's free can't he

James?.......James!

James Yes dear

Jean Oh, I wonder what we can do with these old curtains, they don't seem to match the new carpet you bought us, James. Whatever shall we do? Then there's this parents evening. What dress should I wear? Nothing too boisterous and then there's the other parents to think about. What will they all be wearing? Heaven knows (holding up a dress to herself) Should I wear this one James or the one with the little suit jacket that goes with it, James, James?

(No answer from James who continues to stare downwards at his book)

Jean Should I go and have a look in the shops perhaps?

(no reply)

Jean Oh James, I'm off to the shops, maybe you'll listen to me when I get back

(Jean exits)

James continues to read and after a moment or two he looks up, startled, from the pages of his book as if he has heard something but what amounts in his eyes to just another distraction is easily and soon dismissed and he slumps back down in his chair to continue the slow plod through his book. He loosens his tie a little and seems calm.

Enter Marvin, back from school

Marvin Hi Dad! How's life? I'm just in from another marvellous day at that comprehensive you send me to.

James Well, stick with it and who knows where it will lead you. How are you getting on?

Marvin Fine, except I'm a bit stuck with this computer of mine. It keeps playing up and the time I'm spending on fixing it makes me late handing in assignments.

James glances up and makes eye contact with Marvin but does not otherwise react.

Marvin I just thought I would let you know in case you think I'm slacking when there's work to be done. It's not my fault, it's the computer you see. It keeps playing up.

James Yes. Your sister will be home soon so make sure you've got everything set right in the dining room so she needn't fret when she comes in from work. You know what she's like about work.

(Exit Marvin – he meets Matilda on the way out and acknowledges her in the wings before going off stage completely)

We are left in silence for a moment or two with just the setting of James and his book to entertain us before Jean returns clumping noisily onto the stage.

Jean Oh look James, I've bought it. I've bought just the thing. When the assistant showed me it, I just couldn't resist. It's the pattern, you know. It's just what Sasha was telling me about and showing off in last week, only this is better. This is, well, superior and it challenges you, don't you think. It asks questions, don't you think? I am so lucky to have found such a piece on such reasonable terms.

James How much did it cost, darling?

Jean Oh, a trifle and then there's this other thing that goes along with it. A kind of wrap around that's meant for occasional wear or maybe something for the summer. Look how the patterns mix and match James. They mix and match just like the lady said.

You wait till you see me in it. All those other wives down at the club, wait till they see me in it. They probably won't actually *say* anything but in their hearts they'll be really in awe of me James.

What do you think James? Shall I wear it tonight?

James Do you know how much these things cost?

Jean You can't expect me to take it back now James. Those sort of shops are so touchy about that kind of thing. It's as if you are insulting them on purpose.

Anyway, I happen to know the lady in there and she might even be at the parents evening so you see. I simply can't take it back.

Bookface YES! (booming voice)

James is seen not to react and he clearly hasn't heard a thing. Jean's obvious reaction, nodding an acknowledgement is clear proof that she has reacted unknowingly to the voice.

Both exit the stage at different sides.

Scene 2

We are spectators at the parent's evening Jean and James have been asked to attend. Cheese and wine is available from a buffet table while the parents wait between appointments with the teachers. Present are Jean, James, Dave (a computer repair man), Annabel and other parents

Jean They asked Marvin if he'd like to run the 100 metres for the county. A bit of an honour apparently and he's only fifteen. Some people advance faster than others, I suppose but still I think it's quite an achievement for him. I always knew he'd be good at sport with that physique. It's just knowing how far to push them.

Bookface Yes!!! (booming - only Jean reacts to acknowledge this. The others appear to hear nothing)

James Yes. I quite agree

Jean And I think the teachers here are strong in just that. Then there's Matilda. She's so strong in the arts and sciences, I'm surprised they haven't offered her a scholarship or something. She is so far in advance and she is even technically minded on top of all that. She takes such an interest in computers and suchlike.

Dave Oh, that's interesting. Sorry. I couldn't help overhearing. I'm a computer repair specialist. Perhaps I could help her out. I've got some spare time at the moment while they renovate the office. I'm just here on my own to listen to what they think of my son's progress.

James Really!

Annabel Why, that's wonderful Jean. Did you hear that? This man can help Matilda out with her interest in PC's. You never know where these things can lead. Perhaps she will gain distinction in this area one day

Dave Here's my card. Feel free to give me a call some time

Bookface No!

Jean Oh, are you sure. I really feel that I shouldn't impose. You must be very busy and then there's the finding of free time to consider. I'm so busy these days. We're both so busy. I really must refuse.

Bookface No!

Dave continues to offer the card to Jean

Jean I'll see what Matilda says then (and she takes the card)

Bookface Yes!

James This way darling! We've got more teachers to see.

Annabel I was thinking James, could you find the time to teach Timothy a little in Maths. He's struggling a bit and trying his best to keep up but there's some doubt if they'll let him in to the GCSE. I'm so terribly worried about the whole thing. I really think his future is at stake.

Their eyes meet and James is seen to smile slightly

James Oh, very well Annabel. I'll see what I can do

Jean (suppressing her irritation at their obvious attraction) Good, that's that.

Now come along or we'll be late.

Scene Three

We return to the same domestic scene

Jean Oh James, wasn't that marvellous? Weren't some of the parents simply stunning in their outfits and what a delight it was to listen to them both in their choice of conversation. I felt like a pupil being schooled in the etiquette of parents evening and how they helped me enjoy the evening so much. Oh, and the Neville's. Weren't they just the choicest couple you could ever wish to meet.

Oh, and James! So many people complimented me on my dress. What do you think (and she twirls, allowing the low hem of the dress to swirl a little and show off the shine from the fabric)

James First thing tomorrow, my dear, I want you to take that dress back. Go straight to wherever you got it and tell them it's no use to you and doesn't fit properly. If the worst comes to the worse I can go down there at the weekend and give them a piece of my
mind

Jean Take it back?

Facebook Yes! (Booming) (Again, James is seen not to react)

Jean That's a bit much ! I haven't bought anything for ages. We've been living on not much more than gruel for the last month and I've done my best for all the family and this is what I get in return.

Bookface No!

Jean What do you mean no? Just like that. Well words are cheap. I've got a mind to decide how I like on this one and to leave you guessing. After all I must have some say in our home arrangements. I am your wife you know, in case you hadn't noticed.

Bookface Yes!

Jean Well then, at least we agree on something. I'll make my decision on it in the morning and that'll be that, no discussions.

James Settle down darling

Jean. Yes, that's what I'll do, then I'll go shopping for more oats, lentils and beans and vegetables, yes, vegetables as cheap as you like for us to live for the next few days. You really are most ungrateful James, most ungrateful.... At least I'm slimmer than before, that's all I can say and at least I can fit a dress like that. I don't suppose any of your female colleagues at work would even be half as able as me when it comes to fitting into sheer clothes that flatter them, I'll bet.

Bookface Yes! (at lower volume than before)

Scene Four

Computer problems

Same set in place - James has the day off from work

Marvin: Hi Mum, I think my computer has got a virus

Jean: Well, what can we do about that? We don't know anything about computers and we can't buy a new one can we James ?

James: Yes

Bookface No!

Jean: Well, make your mind up at least. Aren't you late for work?
(No response)

Bookface Yes!

Jean Well, we're on a tight budget. I guessed that much from our chat last night. (She remembers Dave and his card) I'll see what I can do. I might have a contact who can fix it for you Marvin and Matilda can come along for the experience. Now, off you go to school Marvin and forget about it.

Bookface Yes

James: That'll never work

Jean You really are most contradictory you know. One minute you're in favour of something, the next your straight against it. You really must learn to make up your mind.

Bookface Yes

Jean (on her mobile) Hello. David?

David Oh, hi, is that Jean. I though I recognised your voice....charming voice, if I may say so

Jean Oh, thank you. I don't know about that (embarrassed but flattered).

Actually, the reason I rang you is we have a problem with Marvin's computer. You remember Marvin, our son? He's in a panic because he really needs it for his school work. They all do now, don't they?

Dave They certainly do. I know that only too well from my daughter Kelly. Tell you what we could discuss this over a drink at the Four Bells, you know, down by the river.

What do you think?

Bookface No!

Jean Well. I don't know. I hadn't really intended....

Bookface Yes!

Jean Look Dave, I'll see what I can do.

Scene 5

Jean sits alone, centre stage, under the lights. She is pondering something. She speaks.

Jean He's so strange. He never used to be like this. We used to have long discussions. Now he says one thing one minute and another the next. It's the stress at work that's done it. (long pause). You know what I think? I think he's turned into a robot or a computer or something.

Melinda arrives on stage and Jean notices she is there.

Jean From now on Melinda, I'm going to take my own decisions. I'm not going to listen to him anymore.

Melinda Absolutely. Be your own woman if you can. I try to be. I do think you should give him another chance.

Jean One more chance. I'm always giving him chances. He just sits in front of that newspaper barking answers.

Melinda We could test him somehow. See if there's a pattern.

Jean How?

Melinda Speak fast, then say the same thing slowly and see if the answer is the same. I've been looking at him and I think he's got into the habit of not really listening, just replying automatically, alternating 'Yes' and 'No' depending on the speed of the question. We should be able to tell if we test him on this.

Jean Worth a try I suppose.

Scene 6

James is seated and reading the paper as usual. Marvin is also seated, opposite, listening to music on his headphones. A very regular beat is audible and James nods in time. Marvin stops the music and takes his earphones off. He is to join in with the experiment. James continues to nod although there is no music.

Marvin (speaking quickly) Dad, I wonder if you could possibly see your way to buying me a new computer. They've got several on offer down at the shop. We could go down and have a look. I absolutely have to have one for school now. Everybody has one.

James No

Marvin Can I have a new computer? (slowly)

James (no response)

Bookface Yes! (only Jean hears this as usual)

Jean You see, it's just like I said. The man's an automaton. What can I do?

Melinda But mother, you jumped the gun. You must give him time. He could just be ignoring Marvin.

Jean No. When I know something, i'm sure of it and i'm as sure as I can be about this. He's just not there. I don't know how much more of this I can stand. He's not with it and he's so contradictory. In fact, I will make a decision, I have made a decision, I think.

My life is changing.

Melinda Hang on a minute Mum. Don't get upset. My life is changing too. I've chucked my job at the call centre and I'm going on a course. It's funded too. They teach you all about IT. It's quite senior. Soon I'll be able to write programmes and software. The whole bit. So I might even help Marvin with his laptop. So you see, some things are positive. You just need time to think about your options and I'm sure you'll make the right choice.

Jean Well, I'm going out tonight. Dave has asked me for a drink.

Melinda You mean the man from IT4U?

Jean He's a human being as well as being a dab-hand with computers. A very warm and caring human being

Melinda Alright. Cool it. I was only asking. So you'll be out tonight

Jean Yes! (loudly – like Bookface)

James (perking up) Eh... what?

Jean I'll be out tonight James.

James Right

Jean And I'll probably be out for a good few more nights in the near future.

James Right then. (Jean exits) What about the meal?

Scene 7

In the 'Four Bells'. Jean and Dave are sitting outside at one of the tables in the Beer Garden. They are holding hands.

Jean Oh Dave! I don't know. I just can't do this. It feels right being with you but I just feel a responsibility for him.

Dave Well, if you want to spend the rest of your life responding to a machine, shoving you this way and that like a rag doll then that's up to you.

Jean I often feel it's like being married to a computer. You know, how those machines only let you fill in the blanks and in the way they are designed to accept answers. You can't ask questions but just click on a list of options or frequently asked questions.

The software makes mistakes but the computer never admits a fault or responds to the way you want to phrase a question. It always has to be the way it formats it and of course, everything is without any emotional overtones. Is that a good thing?

Dave There, there. Don't get overheated. You may go into emotional meltdown!

(They look into each other's eyes and smile a meekly.)

Jean Oh dear. I think I could get used to this. I'll have to tell James. I really owe it to him.

Bookface Yes!

Jean Yes, I really must.

Dave Don't worry about that. You'll know when the time is right. People need to communicate and if they don't or can't then they have a problem. People will always have emotions *because* they are people but they also need to look at things objectively.

It all depends whose viewpoint you are looking from. And technology could be changed to be more people friendly instead of just improving war capability.

Jean I do love it when you go on! I wish I had such interesting conversations at home. But I must get back. I have to tell James about my decision.

Dave Decision?

Scene 8

Melinda has just returned home. She is tired

Marvin: Hi Melinda. How goes it?

Melinda: Oh, terrible! Everything's scripted. If you go off the script your pay is docked!. I can't wait till I chuck it and start my new job. I actually started chatting naturally to this old geezer and the supervisor came up to me and he was furious . He was going to dock my pay but when he discovered that this geezer was going to put his account with us he backed down. I don't know how long I can stick it. I wish I was a famous artist like Hirst or something. At least they are allowed to think for themselves.

Marvin : Is that the one who did a dead cow or a shark or something **?**

Melinda: Yeah, but at least he did something that meant something. I remember that huge ashtray of cigarette butts he did. It really made you realise how horrible smoking is, just because it was so big....

Marvin: Yeah anyway I'm in a bit of a mess myself. My computer's completely bust and you know what Mum and Dad are like about money, although Dad has been rather strange lately. He actually let Mum go off to buy a dress.

Melinda: No! That's incredible.

James appears upset, wriggles in his chair but continues to read his paper

Marvin: Anyway, do you know anything about viruses Dad ?

James: Yes, actually. The computer can't distinguish between valid information it is asked to disseminate and viruses. It just sends it out to millions of people like you.

Marvin: So I'll have to empty my hard drive and run all my software again

James: No

Marvin :Well what then? (frustrated)

Scene 9

Jean returns from a shopping trip. She has gone with Dave. Dave comes back with her. A confrontation ensues.

Jean: I got this one I saw in Wilson's . Do you like it (holding a dress up)

James Not another dress!

Dave enters

Jean It's for Turkey. Aren't we going to turkey this year? Has it slipped your mind or something?

James: No

Dave Look mate, just 'cos your wife goes out and buys nice things doesn't mean you need to go all bad tempered on her. Most men would be pleased that their partner was at least making an effort, but you.

Jean Aren't we going to Turkey then ?

James: No

Bookface No!

Jean Oh, Dave! Now you see what it's like for me. I can't stand it anymore.

James You won't find me lacking when it comes to caring. You should see what it's like where I work. The way people behave there, you wouldn't believe it. I'm more caring than I should be. All the people at work think so.

Bookface Yes!

Dave Well you're not at work now. This is your wife and family we're talking about and you don't even seem to care. You don't know how lucky you are, sitting in that chair with everything you need at your fingertips. I suppose you think they owe you or something.

Bookface No

Jean Oh Dave, now you see what it's like for me. It's like I'm dealing with a machine. You see, I can't stop reacting to his monosyllabic responses. I have to

leave. I have to leave now. Come with me Dave, come with me.
They rush off the stage together, much to the amazement of the assembled company.

Act 2

Scene 1

Rescue. Jean is walking on the downs. The weather is bad. She wondering what to do with her life.

Jean What am I to do? My life is in tatters. All the decisions I've made and all for what, all because of some voice I'm hearing. It's really no good. I should have had more discretion and decided things of my own accord. I might just as well not exist.

Jean And then there's Dave and my kids. What do I do about them and how do I justify myself to James and the others? What will they think of me? What will I say to James when I meet him again now things have settled down a bit?

She pauses by the cliffs and contemplates throwing herself into the sea below, realising the folly of what she has done, behaving in a way that conforms to the demands of the voice, Bookface.

Jean This is it. I never should have gone with what that voice told me. What am I to do, really, I'm a disgrace in the eyes of this world and everybody in it
She motions to throw herself off but just before she does so she turns round and sees someone approach. It's Dave.

Jean It's you, Dave, it's you! (and she takes a step back from the edge of the cliff).

Dave I was just thinking about you. How are you?

(No reply)

Dave What are you doing out in this weather Jean? Come back. I'll take you home.
in the van.

Jean Nothing will go right at the moment, Marvin's computer has completely packed up. James seems to have forgotten how to talk, he's always buried behind a newspaper, Matilda hates herself or her job or something, and then there's you. I moved out because of you and took the kids with me. We're together when we want to be but for what and for how long Dave?

Dave: Well, I've been working on the business and it's been going very well actually, I could do with some help... My wife's walked out on me since we met so I'm looking after Marianne on my own.

Jean: Oh dear. What a thing for you to face Dave. I don't know how you manage it now your wife's walked out. We only have each other now! I could

Dave, if that's what you want

Dave: Look., thinking about the kids, tell Marvin to bring his computer in and I'll have a look at it on a friendly basis. I'll see what I can do and then at least you'll be able to see that something is getting better. What we do for our kids, eh!

They kiss; firmly *and* romantically.

Jean Yes, of course I'll go with you. I want to go to Bournemouth and live with you and your mother and help set up a branch of IT4U. It sounds idyllic, now that you mention it and no, I don't mind working in the shop, as long as we can go on holiday together.

Dave Come on, I'll drive you home

Scene 2

A New Life.

A party is taking place back in the family home. No one is quite sure of the reason for the party. Jean and Annabel are dancing half-heartedly to Latin sounds. Other people are dancing James sits slightly part from the action and is more and more removed from proceedings.

Melinda Come on Dad! Come and dance. You'll enjoy it when you get into it. Isn't this music just wonderful?

James No thanks (curtly)

Annabel (approaching James) Come on James. You're missing out.

Jean tries physically to drag him up. Eventually he does so and joins them both in a stilting, mechanical dance turning form left to right.

Jean Come on, dance with me at least, for old times sake. Everyone is joining in. It would be a shame if you were the only one to miss out.
The 'Yes', 'No' of Bookface is audible in the background and changes to the beat and rhythm of the music. The family ignore it but James starts moving to the beat and it looks like he's enjoying himself for the first time in ages.

The doorbell rings. (it's Dave)

Dave Oh, Hi. I just thought I would bring the laptop round as I was in the area. I've completely rebooted it and re-installed all the systems so it should be fine so long as Marvin doesn't ..

Jean Oh, that's marvellous. Thanks. Come in and have a drink. They dance so wildly that she slips and twists her ankle. Dave continues dancing and talking about computers and the like.

Jean 'Stop talking nerdish rubbish and 'phone me an ambulance. Can't you see I'm hurt?

Scene 3

All alone

James in his bedsit. Slumped in a chair, trying to concentrate but he is restless and speaks to himself. He is resigned to the fact that Jean is unlikely ever to return and is neutral and monotonous as a result.

James I wonder why Annabel hasn't phoned.

She normally calls on a Monday.

Shall I go bowling instead?. I always liked bowling'

Bookface 'Yes'

James clearly reacts to this and he gets up slowly from his armchair.

James 'In that case..I'll get my bag.'

End

The Acquisition

by Duncan Wallace

and Mary Louise Coulouris

Cast

Robert

The Milkman

The Oracle

The Banker

Philosophers

Academics

A Librarian

The set is a large room, having six windows and a door. Most of the windows are full length and open from floor to ceiling (with shutters). In its most basic form, it is a rectangular space with six exits marked.

Scene 1

Robert has been left alone to look after the house for a few days and is sleeping late. He is on a bed in the corner of the room

Milkman (whistling and the sound of bottles clinking. He approaches the door.)

Ho, hum. There seems no end to this. Just when you think you've done what's asked of you another load comes along and swamps you. (approaches house) I really don't know how much longer I can go on. (turning to the audience). They say your work-shy if you complain but it's not that really, it's the way you have to get up so early and make that part of your routine. Then there's the routine, that's what really gets to you.

There's no magic, no entertainment left here anymore. I used to run at it. Make myself the best milkman on the shift. Tried to win all the praise you know, but after a few years of that you run out of steam and all that's left is the routine and the hard work, yes, the hard work.

(clunks milk bottles down on the doorstep)

Robert (Deep sleep, then wakes suddenly, lifting his head from his bed)

Milkman Up at three every morning rain or shine. Now that is quite something, and driving this cart around. It goes nowhere really and doesn't do nothing for me. It's not like it's a Ferrari or anything with a racing trim. All it's got is milk and orange juice and that and something to make those housewives smile. At least some of them seem pleased to see me.

Them and the cats wot hang around me looking for cast-offs. What am I to make of it, I don't know. No one follows them around waiting for me to say or do something. Hangin' on my every word. All I get is 'yes please' and a 'no thanks' if i'm lucky.

My mother always used to say I had a talent for music and what with that audition I got for the pantomime things seemed to be going places at one time and then I let myself down I suppose. Why didn't I go for it? I might just have dome and then who knows where things might have went. I just got a blank face.

I should have expected it really; all I get are blank faces and short shrift. There must be trouble with my confidence or something. The thing is, with that sort, the urge never leaves you, what is inside is still there and even if they refuse you, you could still go on and all it takes is a bit of encouragement for you to want it and with time you want it all the more. I'll always like a good tune if you know what I mean and when I'm alone, when it's just me and my imagination then I can play out what I could have been..

Never really cut out for it, though, that's where I end up when I sit down after it all. Never really the right shape for the peg-hole if you know what I mean. These people you see on the X-Factor, I don't know how half of them get the nerve, can't sing a note, some of them, so my old mother says. It's embarrassing don't you know.

(Robert hears the milkman clanking and talking outside house and wakes up fully)

Robert At last! Free from the ties that bind and all that debris holding me back. I don't know what it is but I've been feeling weighed down a bit recently. Now uncle Roger's away for a few days and nothing to do but think about what matters and do what I want.

He's left me in full charge and I am always at my best when I'm in charge. That's what the guidance people at school say. That's what my teachers have said about me since primary school.

'Robert likes being at the head of things', and now I am! At last, I can look over what I survey and nothing can move or change without my permission. There isn't even that brother of mine to interfere in the superior way he has. Just cause he's a bit older than me, you would think that royalty had decreed that he act in a certain way towards me and Mum and Dad lapping up and praising all that he does.

(He gets up out of bed and walks around the room)

Haven't seen them for ages. Last time was when they dumped me at my latest school, hoping that I would get on better there away from the bullies and the fanatics and all that. The teachers suggested that my progress might be being affected by my environment and I didn't make any protest so they just went with it. Before setting of for new pastures with Tim, my brother, they took me out of my prep school and dumped my on the local comprehensive.

That was two years ago now and I'm really settled in the new place and over here with my uncle I feel right, like things might go in my favour now that I have moved.

I suppose they're doing all the usual stuff, sticking to the conventions. Dad hammering out his career, Mum caring at home and inspiring my brother to greater things and being quietly satisfied with his progress and not thinking much about the other one, fifty miles away with his uncle. I haven't had time to stop, been breaking new ground, that's what comes out of wildness, that's what I think, that's the end product.

Some of them say I'm an adventurer and a charmer or will be one day so, I ask you, what more is there for me to do or know. The school routine just bores me, always has. There's the art class but that's about it and what about all those teachers. Some of them I like, some I don't.

It's not like they react when I'm there and act all disappointed when I'm not, the light going out of their eyes and their voices dropping. I'll give that a miss for a while and sit back here. (he looks around the room and sits
down)

I'm not going in there to be laughed at because of my obvious intelligence by a group of peers who trash my ideas. Sandra and Ronny, well, they're alright but they don't half tow the line if a clash breaks out and it's their reputations that are on the line.

What the teacher thinks and what the others in class think must be really important to them. Then there's what to do when I'm all alone with Sandra and I think something is about to happen between us and I don't know what to do or think.

Whatever will she make of me, I don't know. Sandra is what makes my world go around and one minute she's there, all sweetness and light, the next she's out of my orbit and I don't know how to act. Makes me a bit unsteady and less sure of myself and my parents have always been against that. Want a steady man to look after things when trouble comes along.

Pushed that on me from an early age they did.

(he walks to the front door, opens it and waves an acknowledgement to the milkman who is by now quite far away, then goes back to the table and swigs down some of the milk)

A holiday is what I need and is what I'm going to take. It's nothing more than I deserve. No more school or friends or thinking about school or friends for a couple of days, just me on my own together with my own collection of thoughts.

A break from it all is just what the doctor ordered, who needs school? Not today

anyway. It'll help me get my ideas out of the jumbled state they're in. Getting things into line is important and anyway I just don't give a damn about what's going on out there.
Look out at the trees and the bushes that's what I say. They're in blossom and the sun is peeking over the horizon already beckoning on another beautiful day, Who needs institutions, schools, factories and reformatories. I don't care for any of it. They won't miss me and I don't miss them.

(Stands up and strolls around room)

I've never really had the chance to check this place out before, loads of books and things and there's uncle Rogers' old hunting knife. What should I make of it all?

I want to know what's in it for me. What's it all about from my perspective? The local highs and lows just aren't doing it for me any more, I need something wider, something from out there that speaks to me or else I'm just gonna go crazy.

There's Sandra but what does she mean to me really and then there's my job down at the centre on a Saturday but that doesn't make up for all the things I've been feeling lately. There's so much to miss and it worries me.

(sits down again)

It seems easy just thinking for today, but I need something much more concrete to move me. Perhaps there is some surprise nobody has told me about yet that's just waiting for me around the corner that will let me just laugh at all this but right now there seems no substitute for breaking those chains and standing up for not doing anything.

All I can do and the best I can do is take some of my own advice and just let things pass in the ordinary way and not get too stressed about. John tells me he's got it all sown up but what does he know? I think he's heading for a train wreck the way things are with him right now and he turns round and hassles me.

(he lies back in his seat)

Yep, there's nothing anyone can really tell me about what's going on. In the end it's up to me, I just wish I knew more than how to make a cup of tea in the morning and how to kiss a girl.

(He stretches then gets up and walks over to one of the shuttered windows and pushes open shutters to let some of the morning light in)

The Oracle

The window opens on a scene in Delphi. It is a summer night with a view of the mountains. Fire lights the face of the oracle, a beautiful woman dressed in classical Greek robes. She is leaning over chanting and throwing some small objects onto a fire that will soon be lit

Robert (breathes in strong perfume and gazes with astonishment on scene). He is lost for words at the pure astonishment of what greets him as he stares out of the window he has opened.

Oracle 'The people of my country are restless and unhappy. I suppose this is natural, as normal as the tendency for the bees to carry pollen. They come in large numbers and want me to predict the future. It is so they can benefit from it and get to where they want to be, achieve their objectives as they say in the other world but they must realise that I am not just here for them.

I have my own ambitions, my own dreams to realise. It makes sense that I can't function without them. People want answers, they demand this from me but I answer them by saying that things must be phrased in my own terms.

Even an oracle has to drink, eat and even smoke you know. I try to explain things in these terms. I hope they will understand the contradiction that is inherent in my state. I can only speak in my own words. This you must know, Robert, this you must know.

Robert (astounded) But... What's all this!? I only opened a window. I must be going mad but I can't drag myself away from it all. It fixes my imagination somehow. What about Robert and school and mum and dad? I can't spend forever here.

Oracle They want me to predict the future and they come in large groups. The times are unsettled and the ordinary folk are unhappy. It's the cause of it all I don't understand. Perhaps I will someday. I remember hearing of my ancestors who had to deal with people with some power to control the city and even they were not at all happy in some cases. Remember to guard against unhappiness whenever it assails you. I can do so at any time and for any number of reasons.

Try to discover what these reasons are before you act as the result of any unhappiness you may feel. You may find that when you look at these reasons, whatever they are, that you are no longer so unhappy and can move on with your life.

Be tender and kind with the women that you meet. Some of them have had no say because they are women and the problems this causes needs to be talked about and explored by all of us, playwrights and athletes alike You listen well Robert, I notice this.

You wait in silence on my word. But why not ask me a question?

Robert I don't know what to say! All of this has come as so much of a surprise. What....who, are you?

Oracle But I could well ask you the same question! The scene you see behind me is of ancient times in Greece where people fought long and hard for what they believed and made others weep at the ferocity of their demands. You are gazing at me and I will tell you that I am the renowned Oracle of Delphi and you are privileged to have the time to spend with me. What would like to ask of me?

Robert Ok then, erm, what does the future hold for me and how should I make the most of it?

Oracle You must listen closely to those around you for they hold the keys from which you may derive some meaning in your life and look to the future. You must see yourself in relation to those around you, not just as a stand alone who wishes that the wind would change in his favour and things would get better for him. This is how you are looking at things at the moment.

This may seem unimportant but there are aspects in all parts of your life that you can make better if you remind yourself that you are more meaningful than you imagine. Others around you are sensitive to this and can begin to make things happen for you.

(scene fades to a cloud of smoke and the oracle disappears)

Robert I wonder what else there is around here. That was amazing. What an experience It's set me thinking. Maybe I'll give Tanya a call and tell her what happened.

Oh, but she'll never believe me, who would. I'll try another window, I need some air anyway.

(and he opens the shutters of a window near the kitchen sink in the open plan room)

The Banker

View of an overfed man pacing back and forth in a large office overlooking the city and a marina. He is speaking on the 'phone.

Banker Hi Ambrose, how are you...good...good. I've been thinking over your points about the flow of credit and leverage in the sub-prime accounts and I really don't think we can move on that...

I've done an analysis of the cross section of the type of client we have and I firmly believe that the smaller accounts are the way to go. I don't care if they have defaulted on their payments in some cases. In this case a broad base of little people add up and mean something. That's what I mean to say to you. So have a think about it and get back to me

(he looks over his shoulder)

Oh, its you. (Looking at Robert who is staring out of the window at the same time).

Well, young sir, don't just stare. What have you come to see me about. It's a bit early in life for you to get involved in the ins and outs of the world of finance. It can't be expected to hold much interest for you know but wait and see what happens in the next few years.

Roger always held out hope that you would join us here one day and make a career out of it but there's a lot of water to flow under the bridge yet between now and then.

Robert I'm not sure what's going on but I could get used to this. I'm having fun. What should I be doing now?

Banker Look at people and do your best to learn from them. That way you won't be as alarmed when it comes to a real situation you have make decisions about. Money comes down to people at the end of the day, you have to know about people and their aspirations and always remember to err on the side of caution.

Things will seem a lot less intimidating that way when it comes to the crunch. Forget about the issues at home and at school and become detached. In that

way you can learn from them and progress.
That will make you better suited for a job here at the bank. You'll be grateful for it one day, just wait and see.

Robert I think I know all that but I'm so unsure about a lot of things, just ask my mates. It's becoming a bit of a crisis for me.

Banker Certain qualities come with time and you should make the most of the time you have now to build relationships and learn a bit about the world. It'll all come in handy in this line of work let me tell you. I have learnt so much from simple experience and it goes a long way when I'm dealing with people from all over the world.

Robert Can I write to you or something?

Banker Look, I'm quite busy, so if there's nothing else just hang in there son and make the most of your opportunities. Try not to squander the chances you do get. Does that make any sense to you?

I've got to get back to my desk, there's a thousand and one
things to get done and it's eleven thirty already.

Robert Thanks, man. (and retreats from the window, closing the shutters as the scene fades or banker exits stage and Robert turns back to face front)

Robert This is getting stranger by the second. (looking up) He even got the time right and everything, like he'd been there all the time for me and I just had to ask. I suppose he's right and I should look at things from a more detached point of view. I could learn but what if I thought too much and things kind of exploded and no one wanted to know me anymore. I could hardly make myself more unpopular and I think I want popularity to guide me through the times I'm in. Oh, I don't know. I'll see if I can clear my brain
with some sleep.

(He settles back in the chair and can soon be heard snoring or seen to be sleeping)

The Philosophers

There is a knock at the door and Robert is woken by it. It is early afternoon and the sun hurts his eyes as he opens the door and looks at the small group of men, some robed, some suited that greet him on the doorstep.

Philosopher 1 Well come on, let us in then. We can't be standing here all day now can we?

(The men assemble around a central table nibbling at the bread and some crisps they have found. One goes and boils a kettle of water for some tea)

Phil 2 You know the Bonacci series, or is it Bocacci, I'm never too sure.

Ph 3 Bonacci I think 3, 5, 8, 13.

Ph 1: The Vienna seccession period was such a fascinating time. I mean, the people that arose out of it like Klimt and Wittgenstein. Such things would just not have been possible in another era.

Wittgenstein: Sorry, did I hear my name?

Ph 2 (continuing) **:** But the writings are surely always that. They are the intellectual produce of one era (and I wont go in to surplus value) taken into another.

Ph 1 : Do you know the Wittgentstein series of silkscreen prints by Paolozzi. Silkscreen, what a beautiful concept!

Ph 3 At last, I see their significance.

Ph 2 Why?

Ph 3 Because they show the link between logic and beauty, proportion and beauty, music and beauty.

Ph 2 Steady on old chap, explain a bit could you for an old buffer like me.

Wittgenstein The Bonaccio series portrays a logical sequence of proportion in numbers, something Wittgenstein would be using in his work, on a much more sophisticated level, and yet it produces a pleasant harmonious art work in Paolozzi. Yes, harmony is something I try to achieve in my own work.

Ph 1 Something we feel strongly about might I add.

Robert What's all this about? (raised voice)

Ph 1 Were having our annual conference. Isn't it marvellous? But were also here for you, Robert. Now have you anything you wish to ask of us. This is your chance.

Robert I want to know what I should do, what I should focus my attention on. I seem to know so much and yet so little and I have little idea of where I am going.

Ph 2 I think I should refer that one to my colleauge.

Ph 3 Well Robert, you should know yourself first of all and know that you know are very small indeed. Only then will you realise that knowledge is vital to you if you are to progress. You must understand that knowledge is important to you.

Robert (contemplatively)When I think about the situations I'm in at school and at home they don't seem to make much sense but I'll try to remember that.

Phil 2 Knowledge is acquired through experience ,young man, so being young yourself ,you have many years before you truly be said to have acquired knowledge..

Phil 1 Ah yes quite right old boy. Where do correct ideas come from- I believe I wrote something about that myself.

Phil 3 Yes, but you can work out things yourself, with logic in its purest form without moving a muscle, without even moving a muscle

Wittgenstein Ah, but that only goes so far, there's nothing like getting out and about down to the cinema, perhaps to get the mind stirring, tone up the muscles of thought and dream a little.

Robert's has been darting back and forth between the philosophers, listening to their bits of advice.

Academics

The philosophers finish chatting and eating and file out, organised, closing the door behind them. As they recede into the distance Robert slumps back in his chair shocked and confused by all that has happened. He walks over to the door to ensure it is shut then goes over to one of the windows and opens the shutters for some fresh air. Looking out, two men can be seen, seated at a table below. They are debating.

Ac 1 Look, just because it states in the Bible that you shall have no other Gods before me does not mean that you cannot make statues and icons that are worthy of devotion.

Ac 2 Your being too broadminded. Scripture doesn't generally allow for the broad interpretation you are giving it. You cannot grant licence to those who lack understanding and motivation for the true spirit of the scripture.

Ac1 History is on my side. Look at all the legends and stories behind the objects of devotion scattered throughout Europe. Where would be without all of those?

And then there's the happiness and security they give people, they allow them to focus their thoughts on something.

Ac2 Your being too liberal I tell you!

Robert What are you discussing?

Ac1 Oh, nothing really. Just passing the time. And who are you?

Robert I'm at home on my own looking after the place for my uncle Roger who is away on business. I'm finding the time to think about my future. Very useful really.

Ac2 Come and see us up at Oxford one of these days. I'm sure you would like it up there. Plenty of diversions and plenty to think about. Just the thing for a young man like you. Stimulate and broaden the mind. That's what we can do for you.

Ac1 Play any sports do you? Well we cater for that aswell. Put your name down with your school and work hard for those exams and we'll see what we can do.

We go by results in the main, but what school you went to can play a part in the interview.

Robert Well, what's worth trying for? I lack the motivation to work really hard like some people in my class. They're the swots so maybe you won't be seeing the likes of me up there in any case. I'm not that interested in much more than my girlfriend and my job at the moment.

Ac2 It's important that you try hard now and when you can get there you can begin to enjoy yourself more. Put the effort in now and it will pay dividends later. (Robert closes the shutters and walks back across to the chair)

Shrine

He has fallen asleep and when he wakes, realises that it is dark outside and goes over to another window to look out into the garden. In the garden there is a shrine with candles burning and a photograph of one of his classmates in the wooden housing.

Robert What can this be? A wooden box and a candle and a crucifix and there's a photo of Theresa. Oh my, something must have happened to her or is something going to happen to her. Who knows? I wonder what all this is about.

It certainly grabs your attention. Now I remember, there was that road accident last year and Theresa never really recovered and now, well, she must be dead. Oh my God, what's happening. I really liked her and now she's gone. (the wind blows and the candles flicker. Robert keeps staring)

I don't know how to react or what to do. It makes me feel so inadequate all of a sudden.

Yes, now I don't have the answers and I don't know what I should do. Perhaps I should kneel down in front of it to pay my respects. Yes, that's what I'll do.

(His eyes lower to the art work and the signatures of pupils underneath. He keeps staring for some time. Sandra appears beside him)

Robert Sandra! What are you doing here?

Sandra I'm here to make sure you're alright. It must be a bit of a shock to you. To find out something like this and to have no one to back you up. I lost a friend once and I know what it's like. I'm here for you Robert.

Robert This is all so new, I don't know what to think. Does this mean you care about me?

Sandra I care about you and want to be with you. You can't imagine how much I care about you.

Robert This is all a bit of a shock. I want to think about things.

(He retreats back inside the house, closing the shutters)

Library

Robert crosses the room and opens one final window opening onto a library and a librarian.

Librarian Well, come in then. Hop over that barrier there and come in. Robert obliges by clambering through the window and jumping onto to the soft carpet of the library floor.

Librarian Come and see the catalogue. There's every chance we've got just what your looking for.

Robert Wow, that's certainly a list I'm interested. There's everything here from Astrophysics to Zoology and that's just scratching the surface! There's a bit here on relationships in adolescence. Maybe I should have a look at that. Robert thumbs through some of the books and begins reading. Time passes and the new day dawns. We hear the clanking of bottles. It's the milkman again. Robert clambers back through the window and runs to the door and catches the milkman by the arm.

Robert I'm going to be a thinker, you know. I've decided. That's what I want to be. Someone who gets things done. Not just someone who contemplates but who gets things done. And when I've done that i'm going to settle down and get married to the girl I'm in love with!

Milkman (astonished) Are you now son, are you?

End

Epilogue

The Persuaders

Robert and Sandra are walking hand in hand in the country when approached by two men with beards in exotic garb. Flowing eastern robes and very colourful.

Persuader 1 You do realise that to walk over and across that access road back there was a trespass under the relevant Act of Parliament, section three and that consequently you have committed a criminal offence.

Persuader 2 Albeit inadvertently.

Persuader 1 But an offence is an offence all the same, however inadvertent.

Persuader 2 Don't worry. It's how you feel that we are more interested in.

About that and other things. I mean, for all we know you may have dropped litter or had a row that disturbed the peace in the past few weeks and how should you feel then.

Robert Look..

Persuader 1 We know how the ordinary person would feel and how we would feel but the question really is how you would react. Are you part of a commonality where the rules for conduct in life are generally accepted and feelings of guilt when rules are broken and the action one should take are also accepted.

Persuader 2 Are you one of us, we mean, one of humanity where we accept things about ourselves and the action we should take to remedy our transgressions or are you not.

Sandra We didn't mean to walk across the access road. It was a mistake.

Persuader 1 Well, on this occasion if you just give us your phone number and we can stay in touch and check to see if you make any more mistakes and do things you really shouldn't.

Persuader 2 Yes, perhaps you may feel obliged to call us if you have made any further errors that shouldn't be overlooked. Now your grown, you must take responsibility you know.

Persauder 1 Goodbye for now.

www.ingramcontent.com/pod-product-compliance
Ingram Content Group UK Ltd.
Pitfield, Milton Keynes, MK11 3LW, UK
UKHW020229250726
13967UKWH00001B/273

9 781471 033179